This book is dedicated to two very special people.

Firstly, to my late Grandmother Esther Silverman
who planted the seed that many years later inspired
me to produce this book.

Secondly, to my little boy Aaron, who does
not like to brush his teeth.

Tom was a cheeky, cheerful and chatty little boy.

He was a good student, liked playing football and always offered to play with his little sister and walk the dog.

However, Tom had one big problem. He HATED brushing his teeth. He hated it so much that no amount of encouragement from his parents would ever get him to do it.

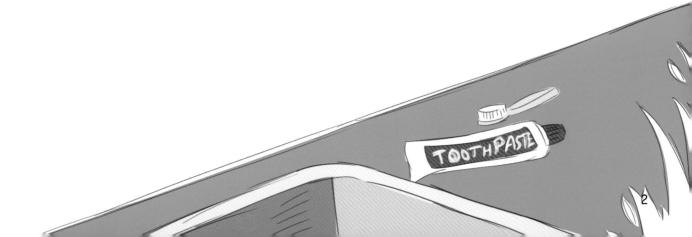

Tom's parents didn't know what to do. They had tried EVERYTHING to help Tom to brush his teeth.

They tried showing him photos of horrible teeth that didn't get brushed which were all yellow and gunky. They tried creating a sticker chart with a big reward at the end, and they even tried brushing his teeth whilst Tom was asleep, but he jumped up shouting "NO NO NO," and closed his mouth tightly.

4

One night Tom was asleep having a marvellous dream when he was woken up by a RA-TA-TAP-TAP noise on his bedroom window. He didn't want to open his eyes because he was enjoying his dream so much, but the RA-TA-TAP-TAP was disturbing him, so he rolled himself out of bed to see what was making all the noise.

Tom walked to his bedroom window, opened the curtains and got a big shock. He thought the moon was right outside.

When Tom took a closer look, he saw a big smiling mouth and two large kind eyes in a yellow moon shaped face staring right back at him.

Tom rubbed his eyes to make sure he wasn't still dreaming, and when he opened them again he heard the moon face saying, "Well, are you going to say hello or not dear boy?"

Tom thought he'd better not be rude, so he introduced himself. "Hel... Hello," he said.

"Splendid my boy, good evening Master Tom, my name is Mr Moony," said Mr Moony.

Tom wondered how Mr Moony knew his name, but his thoughts were interrupted when Mr Moony said, "I'm here to help teach you something you seem to be struggling with, now please find a parent and ask them if they will join you on our wonderful adventure. Then hop into the Moon Express, and don't forget your slippers and dressing gown, it's a bit chilly out here."

Tom didn't know what was going on, but he was always up for an adventure, so he ran out of his bedroom and bumped into his father.

Tom excitedly explained all about Mr Moony, and asked his father if he would join him on a wonderful adventure.

Tom's father agreed, so they grabbed their slippers and dressing gowns and jumped out of Tom's bedroom window, landing comfortably inside a compartment on the Moon Express.

The Moon Express shot straight upwards. "Hold on tight," announced Mr Moony loudly, as he stood in the drivers compartment.

Before Tom could finish shouting, "MR MOOOOOONNNNNNYYYYY," the Moon Express had settled gently on the moon.

Tom couldn't believe it, he had always wanted to go to the moon, and here he was. His eyes widened in excitement when he saw the earth from space, with all its lands and oceans; it was amazing.

"WOW, what a view," Tom and his father said in astonishment.

Tom saw that there were other children and adults climbing out of different compartments from the Moon Express.

"Come on now children and adults please follow me, splendid, righty ho, hippity hop and off we go," announced Mr Moony, so they all followed Mr Moony who led the way.

Tom looked up, and coming into view was an amazing house that looked like it had grown straight out of the moon.

"Now single file please," Mr Moony said as he opened the door of the house, and one by one they all entered.

Immediately, the most delicious smell of freshly baked chocolate chip cookies filled their nostrils, and Tom's tummy began to rumble.

Oh yummy, thought Tom. "Mr Moony sir, where can I get a cookie from please?" he asked.

Just then a friendly looking lady appeared holding a large tray of warm chocolate chip cookies. Tom rubbed his tummy which growled even louder, he really wanted a cookie.

"Oh goody, hello children, it's so nice to meet you all, my name is Mrs Moony, and I have baked some yummy chocolate chip cookies for you all," she said.

Mr Moony loudly cleared his throat and said, "Thank you Mrs Moony, as always the cookies smell delicious, but the children can only get their cookies after they have learnt their important lessons."

"Oh Mr Moony, go on then, but I can't promise I won't eat them all up myself before the lessons are over," giggled Mrs Moony.

"Now now my dear, don't eat them all up at once, we would like to have some delicious cookies too," laughed Mr Moony whilst tapping his tummy.

Mr Moony turned back to the children and instructed them what to do next. "Righty ho," he said, "Could Tom and his father be so kind as to follow me, and would the others please go with Mrs Moony."

Ok, **Tom thought,** *I'd better do as I'm told if I'm ever to get my hands on one of those yummy cookies.*

Tom and his father followed Mr Moony down the corridor which was full of different coloured doors.

"Aha splendid, here we are," exclaimed Mr Moony as he pushed open a red door.

Tom and his father followed Mr Moony through the door and into a room that looked like a dentist's surgery. *Hmmm,* thought Tom, *I hope Mr Moony isn't going to try and clean my teeth, because I won't let him.*

Tom's father took a seat in the corner.

"Now Tom," said Mr Moony as he was getting into a white dentist's coat, "here is your white coat, that should fit very well, do put it on please and let's start with our first patient."

Just then there was a knock at the door. "Come on in," answered Mr Moony. In walked a tall smiling man. Tom noticed he had the most perfect set of sparkling white teeth.

"Aha, welcome Mr Shine," said Mr Moony. "Mr Shine, please meet Tom and Tom's father."

Tom waved a little shyly.

"Come come Mr Shine," said Mr Moony whilst tapping the dentist chair, "please have a seat."

"Tom," said Mr Moony, "would you please pass me the little dentist mirror." Tom looked down at the tray of different dental instruments and located the little mirror on a long stick.

"Here you go Mr Moony," said Tom as he handed the mirror over to him.

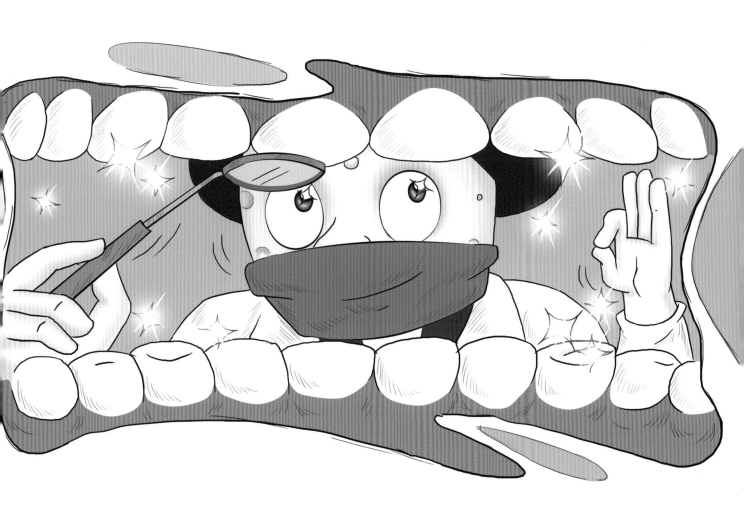

"Thank you dear boy," said Mr Moony, then turning back to have a good look into Mr Shine's mouth Mr Moony exclaimed, "Oh bravo, splendid, what lovely clean teeth you have Mr Shine, do you brush them twice a day?"

"Oh yes," answered Mr Shine. "Every morning after I wake up and every evening before bed, with a large dollop of toothpaste. I also floss and use mouthwash."

"Perfecto, you have set a wonderful example to young Tom here, well done," said Mr Moony, and turning back to Tom he said, "See Tom, what a little brushing and care of your teeth can do, wonderful, splendid, thank you Mr Shine, we will see you again next year."

Mr Shine got up, gave a little bow and disappeared out of the red door.

"Now," said Mr Moony, "we're ready for our next patient."

Suddenly, there was a knock at the door.
Tom looked up and saw that Mr Moony had put a large washing peg on his nose. *Oh, I wonder why he put a peg on his nose,* thought Tom, but just then a horrible smell reached Tom's nostrils. It smelled like rotting cabbages.

YUCK, thought Tom, just as Mr Moony said, "Ahh Mrs Sunny, hello, please meet young Tom and Tom's father, how very kind of you to come, please have a seat on the dentist chair and let's have a look at your teeth."

Mrs Sunny settled down on the dentist chair and gave Tom a big smile. Tom couldn't help but gasp at what he saw. Most of Mrs Sunny's teeth were black and surrounded by thick yellow gunk, and the smell was just so stinky. Tom didn't want to seem rude, so he smiled back and waited for instructions from Mr Moony.

"So Mrs Sunny, I see we don't seem to be having much success with teeth brushing now do we, tut tut," frowned Mr Moony.

Mrs Sunny looked down sheepishly and said, "I'm sorry Mr Moony, I just don't like to brush my teeth."

"Well," said Mr Moony, "I'm afraid we're going to have to take some of these teeth out and clean up the rest as best we can, now lie back and close your eyes, we have a lot of work to do."

About an hour and half later Tom was exhausted and poor Mrs Sunny had to have 5 teeth removed, but at least the awful smell had gone.

"You will remember to brush your teeth twice a day, floss and use mouthwash, won't you Mrs Sunny?" instructed Mr Moony.

"Ok Wista Wooey, I will fwy and bwuth my feef thummore," mumbled Mrs Sunny, who struggled to speak because her mouth was all numb.

"See you again soon and thank you for coming," said Mr Moony.

Slowly Mrs Sunny left the room.

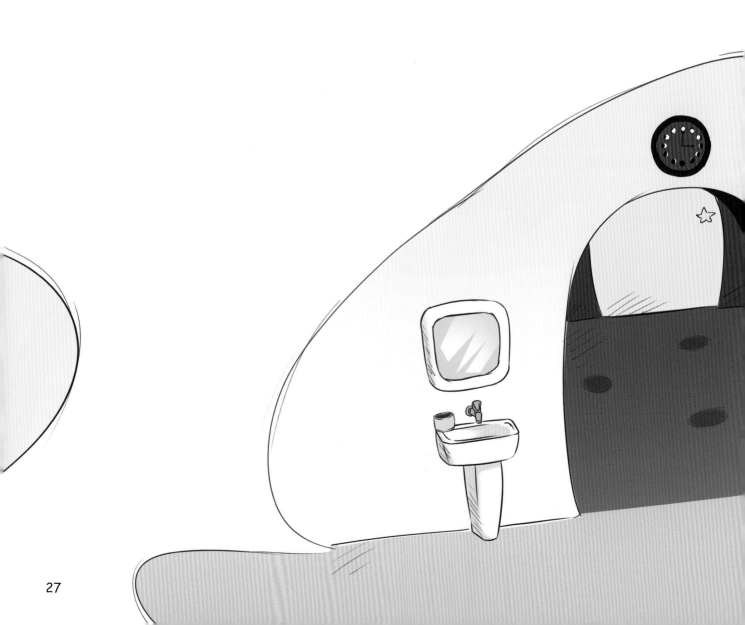

Tom looked up at Mr Moony and said, "I think I know what all this is about, and I promise I will brush my teeth twice a day, use floss and mouthwash starting from now."

"Jolly good," said Mr Moony, whilst handing Tom a small tube of toothpaste, a new toothbrush, some floss and a bottle of mouthwash.

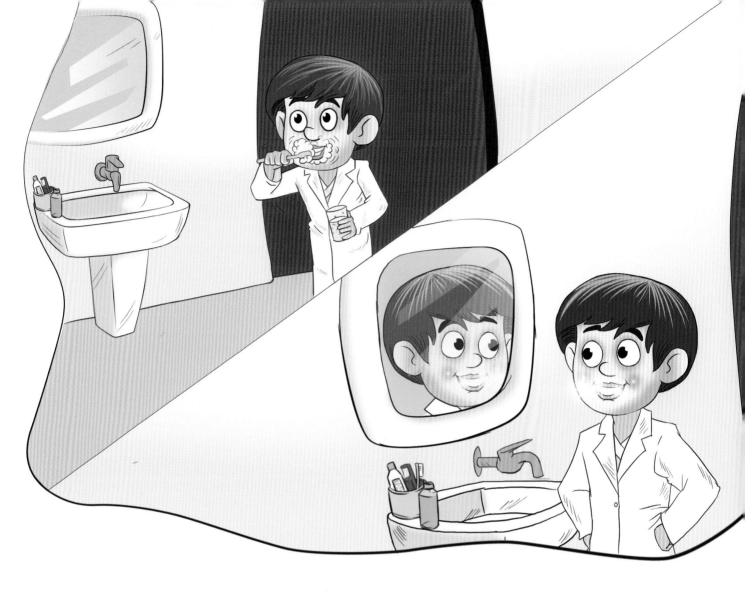

Tom walked over to the sink and started to brush his teeth.
When he finished using floss and gurgling with the mouthwash, he examined his teeth in the mirror and was so excited to see his white sparkling teeth shining right back at him.

"Wow, my mouth is feeling so clean and fresh," Tom exclaimed excitedly, as he walked over to show his father.

"Now that didn't feel so bad did it, splendid and jolly good show," said Mr Moony, who was smiling down at Tom looking proud.

Mr Moony, Tom and Tom's father walked out of the dentist surgery and back towards the dining room. There set out on the table were the scrumptious chocolate chip cookies and a big glass of milk.

Tom was so excited to eat the cookies, but first he thanked Mrs Moony and then he sat down and ate the best chocolate chip cookies he had ever tasted.

After a while Tom heard Mr Moony announce, "Chop-chop children and parents, we have to head back to the Moon Express, it's almost morning time."

The children and their parents thanked Mrs Moony then followed Mr Moony back to the Moon Express and took their seats.

Mr Moony called out, "Hold on tight," and the Moon Express zoomed straight back down towards Earth.

Tom closed his eyes tightly.

Tom slowly opened his eyes and saw that he was back in his room, lying on his bed.

Tom saw that next to him on his bed, sat a small bag full of Mrs Moony's chocolate chip cookies.
In his hands he found a new toothbrush and an unopened tube of toothpaste, and on his bedside table stood a bottle of mouthwash and a little container of tooth floss.
Wow, thought Tom, *so maybe it wasn't all a dream.*
Tom now knew what to do to keep his teeth white and squeaky clean.
"Jolly good show," he chuckled to himself.

Mr Moony & The Little Boy
Who Wouldn't Brush His Teeth

Written by Susan Saleh
Illustrated by Illustrations Hub
Edited by Rob Daniel

Email: mrmoonybooks@hotmail.com

ISBN: 9781916362406

www.mrmoonybooks.com

https://www.facebook.com/groups/mr.moony.books/

ABOUT THE AUTHOR

SUSAN SALEH

I am a children's author living in London, running a busy house with our four children, (two girls 16 and 14, a son of 21 and another son who is 7 and has high functioning autism) dogs, horses and one loving and supportive husband. The inspiration for Mr Moony originally came from my grandmother, who used to smile and tell me when I was little that if I didn't behave then Mr Moony would come and see me. She would tell me little stories about the Mr Moony in her imagination, so I have elaborated and extended these ideas into a friendly and helpful Mr Moony, someone who wants to help children get over their bad habits, fears and phobias in positive ways.

This is the first in a series of Mr Moony books, the second has already been written and is currently being illustrated.

I am writing these books to help deal with the many issues we all go through while raising children, in a fun and informative way. Daily battles with things such as teeth cleaning, fussy eating, cleaning their rooms, doing homework, the list is endless. I hope you enjoy these books as much as I have enjoyed creating them.

I invite you to join our FREE group, come in and have a chat over tea or coffee. The virtual kettle is always on.
https://www.facebook.com/groups/mr.moony.books